Stick

The Very Hungry Caterpillar's
NATURE
Sticker & Colouring Book

Your adventure
starts here!
Can you find a sticker of

The Very Hungry
Caterpillar

to stick on this leaf?

This book belongs to ....

PUFFIN

Rise and Shine

**The sun comes up each morning.
Can you use your stickers to fill the sky
with early birds and fluffy clouds?**

cock-a-doodle-doo

Can you find a sticker of the noisy bird who wakes everybody up?

Stick

Colour

Colourful Critters

Nature is full of mini-beasts!
Can you use your stickers to find the missing bugs?

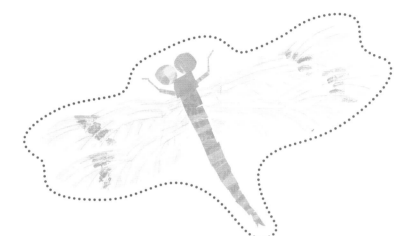

Dragonfly

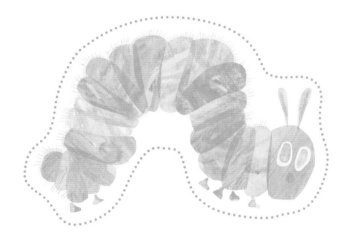

Caterpillar

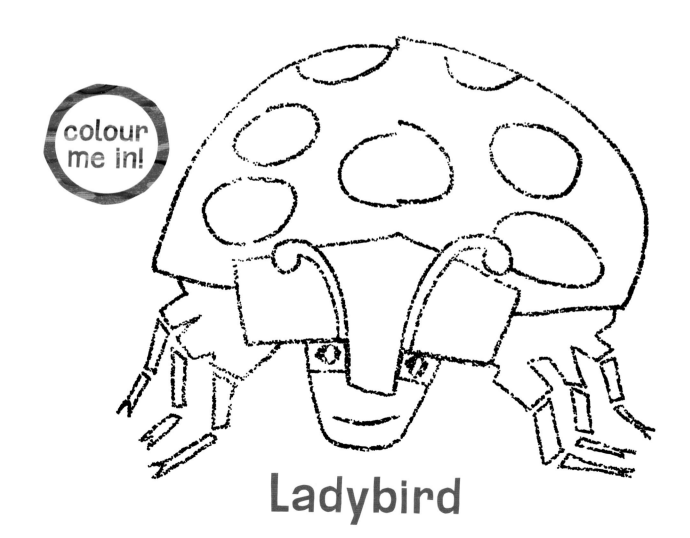

colour
me in!

Ladybird

4

Ant

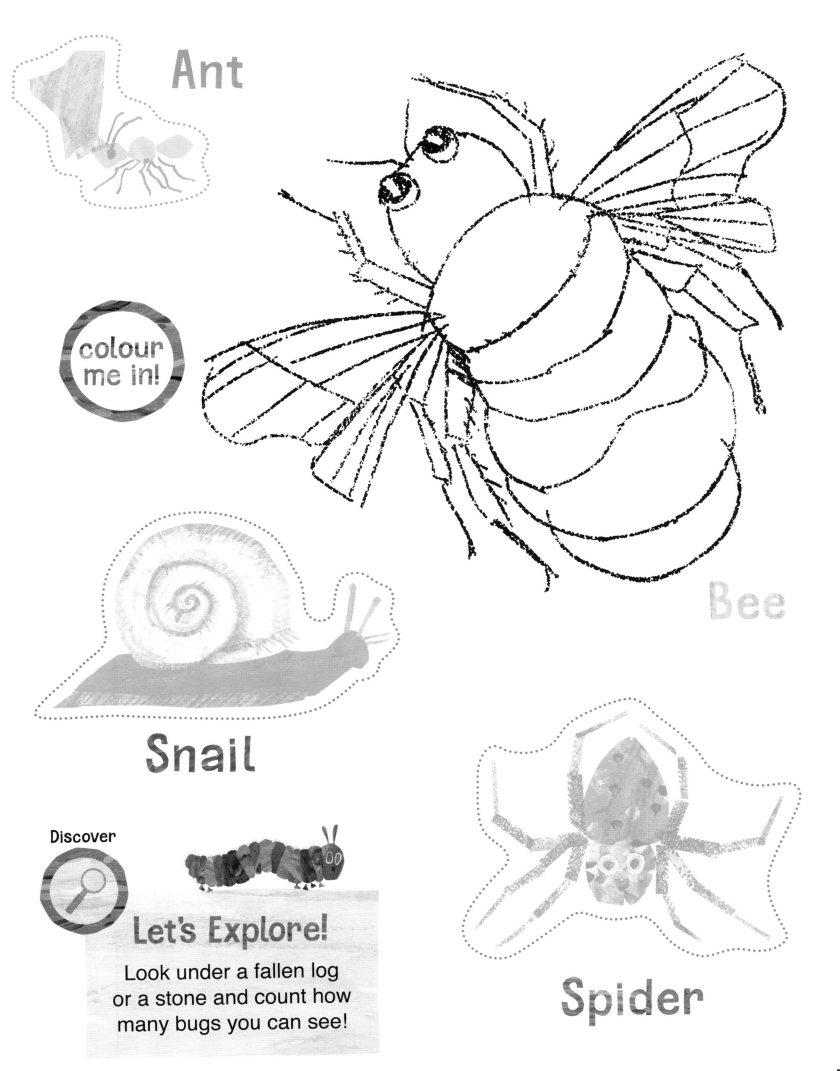

colour me in!

Bee

Snail

Discover

Let's Explore!

Look under a fallen log or a stone and count how many bugs you can see!

Spider

A Flower Story

A flower grows from a tiny seed.
Can you use your stickers to tell the story?

1

A tiny **seed** is planted in the soil.

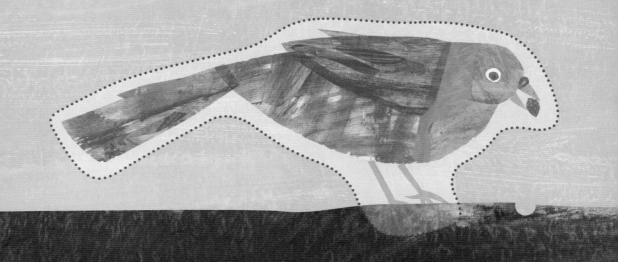

2

It needs water and sunshine to grow.

The little seed starts to grow **roots** in the soil.

3

Its **stem, leaves** and **flower bud** shoot up towards the sun.

4

Then a beautiful **flower** opens up to the sunshine.

5

Later, the wind blows the flower's new **seeds** off and our story starts again.

Busy Bees

Bees collect nectar from flowers to make honey.

Can you find a big sticker of a bee to put in the middle of this flower? Then add some bees buzzing around the flower.

Flower

Bee

Discover

Guess What?

Bees work very hard! Together, 12 bees make 1 teaspoon of honey in their lives. That's enough for just 1 piece of toast!

Beehive

Can you find little bee stickers and put them around their beehive home?

Bees keep their honey in honeycombs. Can you use your stickers to complete this honeycomb?

Honeycomb

Stick

Up in the Trees

Trees are made up of many different parts.
Can you use your stickers to complete this tree?

Leaves

Branches

Trunk

Roots

Stick

Seasons Change

There are four seasons in a year. Can you use your stickers to show how a tree changes in each season?

Spring →

Fresh new leaves grow and sometimes flowers appear.

← Summer

The leaves are green and bushy and sometimes fruit grows on branches.

Page 1

It's time to explore nature with
The Very Hungry Caterpillar!

Page 2–3 – Rise and Shine

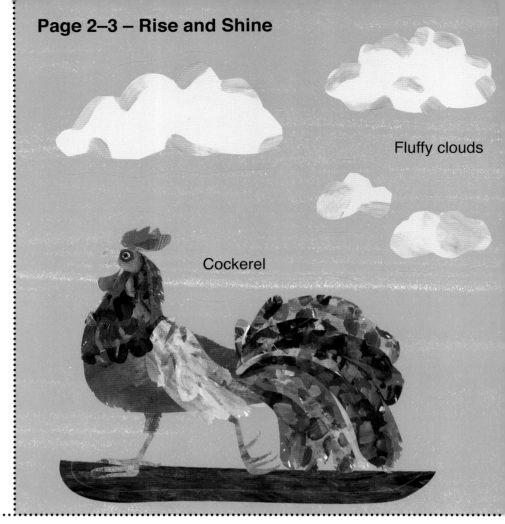

Fluffy clouds

Cockerel

Page 4–5 – Colourful Critters

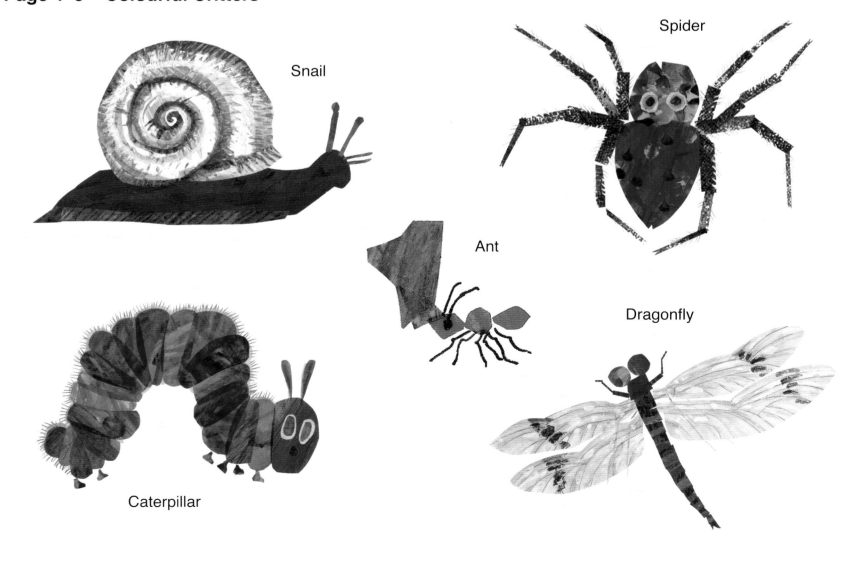

Snail

Spider

Ant

Dragonfly

Caterpillar

Early birds

age 6–7 – A Flower Story

1

4

5

3

2

age 8–9 – Busy Bees

Add these buzzing bees around the flower.

Can you stick these busy bees around their beehive?

Can you put this big bee in the middle of the flower?

Can you fit these missing stickers to complete the honeycomb?

Page 10–11 – Up in the Trees

Trunk

Leaves

Page 12–13 – Seasons Change

Spring

Summer

Page 14–15 – Nature Noises

Owl

Cricket

Duck

Pigeon

Branches

Roots

Winter

Autumn

Cat

Bee

Frog

Mouse

Continued on next sticker sheet . . .

Page 14–15 – Nature Noises
(continued)

Bird

Page 18–19 – A Caterpillar Story

1

5

3

4

Page 16–17 – Wonderful Weather

Add this cloud to the raindrops.

Add the sunshine.

Page 20–21 – Beautiful Butterfly

Bats

Owls

Mouse

Hedgehogs

Fox

Cricket

Fireflies

Fox

age 24 – Twinkle Twinkle

Reward sticker for this book!

I have completed
The Very Hungry
Caterpillar's
NATURE
Adventure

Reward sticker for you to wear!

I have completed
The Very Hungry
Caterpillar's
NATURE
Adventure

Which moon
shape do you
like best?

Autumn

The leaves turn red, gold and brown, and fall to the ground.

Winter

The branches are bare, without any leaves.

Discover

Let's Explore!

Next time you are outdoors, count how many different leaf shapes you can see.

Stick

Draw

Nature's Noises

Can you use your stickers to find these noisy animals?

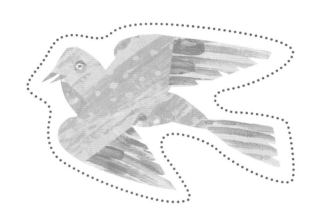

quack

tweet

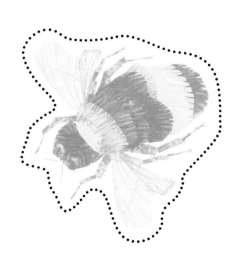

ribbit

meow

buzz

Next, can you match each animal to the noise it makes?

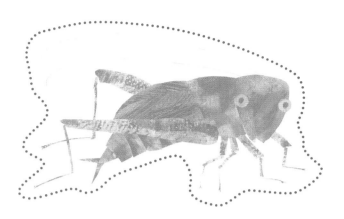

hoot

coo

squeak

chirp

Stick

Colour

Wonderful Weather

Sometimes, when it's rainy and sunny at the same time, a rainbow appears. Can you use your stickers to add rain and sun to the sky? Then use your favourite colours to colour in this rainbow.

RED   ORANGE   YELLOW   GREEN   BLUE   INDIGO   VIOLET

Stick

Colour

A Caterpillar Story

**This life cycle is one of nature's most magical changes.
Can you use your stickers to complete the story?**

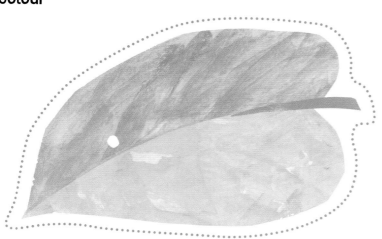

start here

1

A little egg sits on a
leaf.

2

The Very Hungry Caterpillar
hatches.

5

A beautiful
butterfly

emerges from the cocoon.
One day, it might lay an egg
and the story starts again.

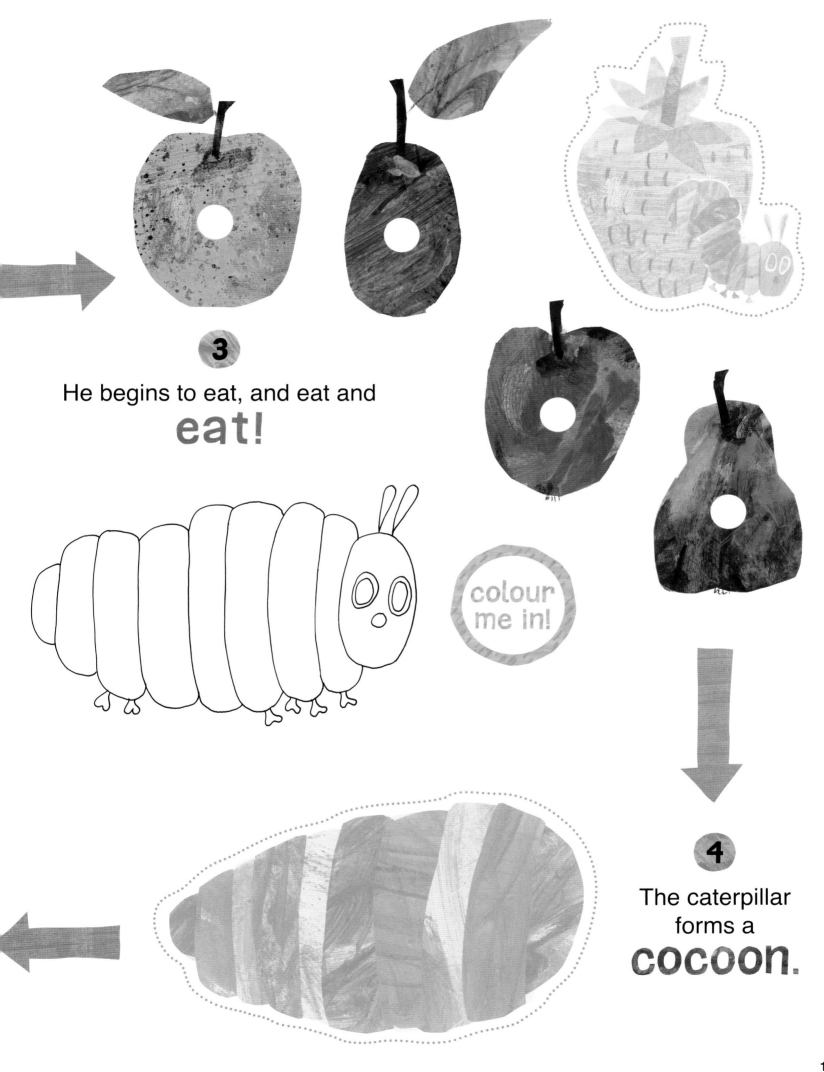

3

He begins to eat, and eat and
eat!

colour
me in!

4

The caterpillar
forms a
cocoon.

Stick

Colour

Beautiful Butterfly

**Can you colour in this brilliant butterfly
with your favourite colours?
Next, use your stickers to decorate.**

Discover

Guess What?

Many butterflies can taste
leaves with their feet!

Night-time Animals

Some animals wake up when everyone else goes to sleep.
Can you fill this scene with night-time animal stickers?

Stick

Stick

Twinkle Twinkle

The moon and stars come out at night.
Can you choose a moon sticker for the sky
and then fill the sky with stars?

I have completed
The Very Hungry
Caterpillar's
NATURE
Adventure

Well done!

Can you find your very
special stickers? You can
stick one here and wear
the other one with pride!